Don't miss the Brown Bear and Friends Audio CD with all four books read by Gwyneth Paltrow!

And look for the hardcover and board book editions of these popular books:

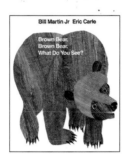
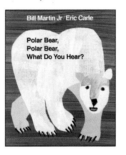

The Eric Carle Museum of Picture Book Art was built to celebrate the art that we are first exposed to as children. Located in Amherst, Massachusetts, the 40,000-square-foot museum is the first in the United States devoted to national and international picture book art.

Visit www.carlemuseum.org

A Note on Endangered Species

We are losing our animals. More than 5,000 animal species are endangered or threatened worldwide. This means that they are in danger of disappearing forever.

To safeguard these animals, there are over 3,500 protected areas in the form of parks, wildlife refuges, and other reserves around the world. This book features ten of these endangered or threatened species.

We can all help save them by spreading the word about conservation.

The author wishes to thank Michael Sampson for his help in the preparation of this text.

Henry Holt and Company, LLC
Publishers since 1866
175 Fifth Avenue
New York, New York 10010
mackids.com

Henry Holt® is a registered trademark of Henry Holt and Company, LLC.
Text copyright © 2003 by Bill Martin Jr
Text copyright © 2004 by the Estate of Bill Martin Jr
Illustrations copyright © 2003 by Eric Carle
All rights reserved.

Library of Congress Cataloging-in-Publication Data available.

First hardcover edition—2003
This paperback edition (2011) not for individual sale.

Printed in May 2011 in the United States of America
by Worzalla Publishing Company Inc., Stevens Point, Wisconsin

10 9 8 7 6 5 4 3 2 1

Panda Bear, Panda Bear, What Do You See?

By Bill Martin Jr
Pictures by Eric Carle

Henry Holt and Company · New York

Panda Bear,
Panda Bear,
what do you see?

I see a bald eagle
soaring by me.

Bald Eagle,
Bald Eagle,
what do you see?

I see a water buffalo
charging by me.

Water Buffalo,
Water Buffalo,
what do you see?

I see a spider monkey
swinging by me.

Spider Monkey,
Spider Monkey,
what do you see?

I see a green sea turtle
swimming by me.

Green Sea Turtle,
Green Sea Turtle,
what do you see?

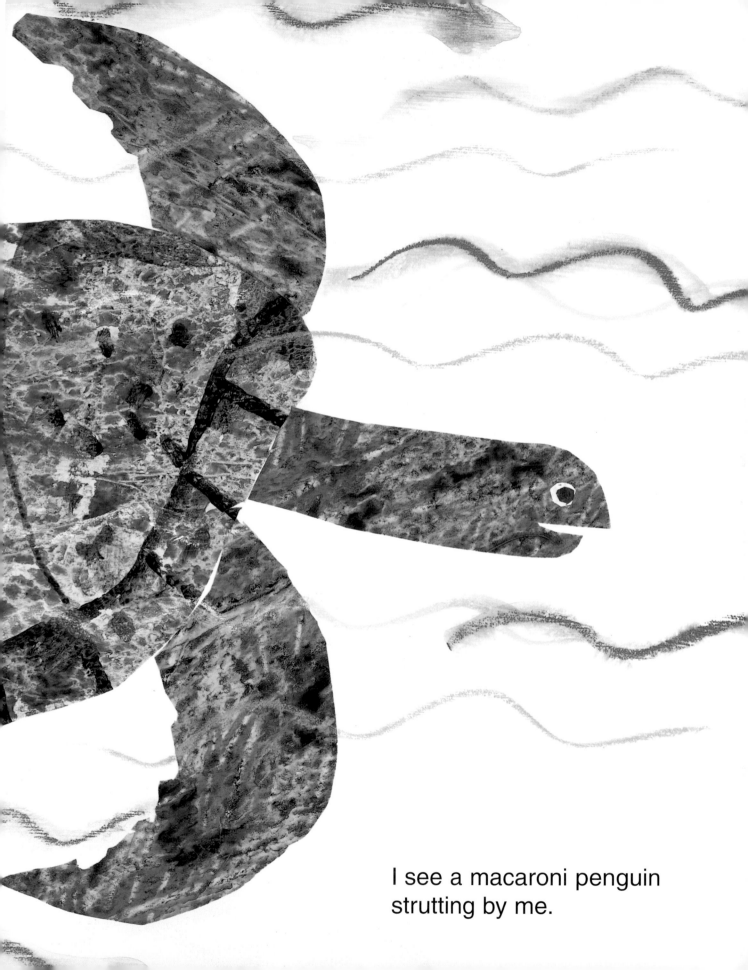

I see a macaroni penguin
strutting by me.

Macaroni Penguin,
Macaroni Penguin,
what do you see?

I see a sea lion
splashing by me.

Sea Lion,
Sea Lion,
what do you see?

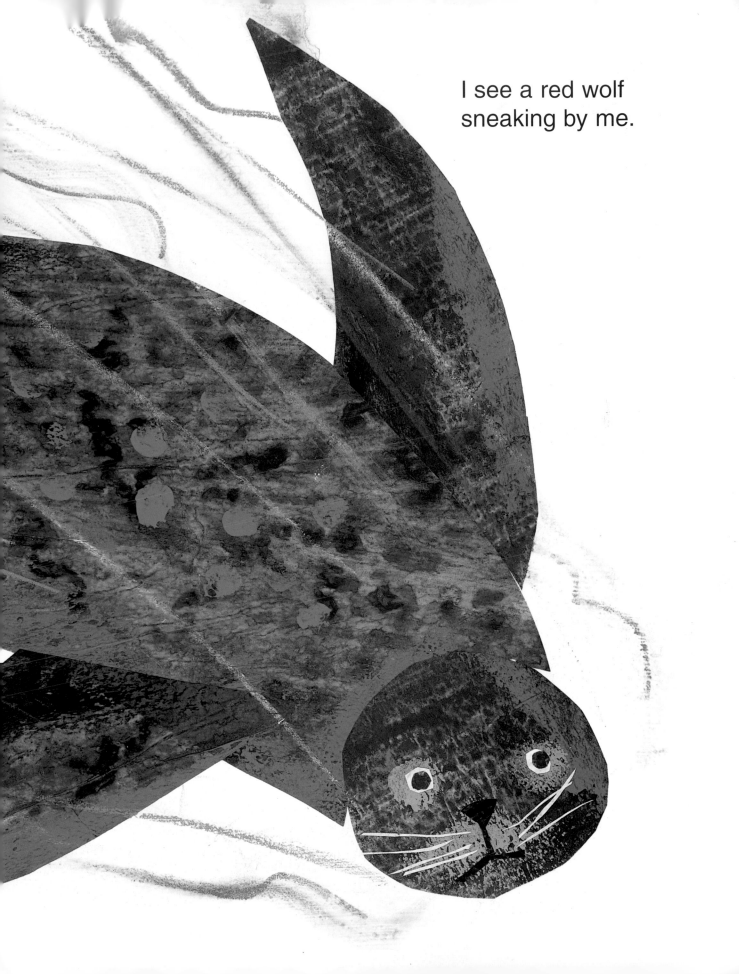

I see a red wolf
sneaking by me.

Red Wolf,
Red Wolf,
what do you see?

I see a whooping crane
flying by me.

Whooping Crane,
Whooping Crane,
what do you see?

I see a black panther
strolling by me.

Black Panther,
Black Panther,
what do you see?

I see a dreaming child
watching over me.

Dreaming Child,
Dreaming Child,
what do you see?

I see . . .

a panda bear,

a spider monkey,

a green sea turtle,

a red wolf,

a whooping crane,

a bald eagle,

a water buffalo,

a macaroni penguin,

a sea lion,

and a black panther . . .

**all wild and free—
that's what I see!**